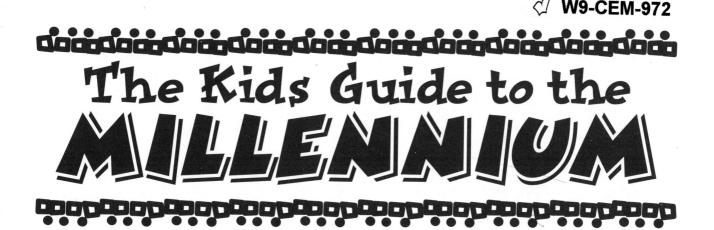

The Kids Guide to the MILLENNIUM

Written by
Ann Love & Jane Drake

Illustrated by
Bill Slavin

Kids Can Press

For Jim and David

ACKNOWLEDGMENTS

Mme Anissa Bachir; Kathleen and Henry Barnett; Neil Beatty; Julie Booker; Paulette Bourgeois; Trish Brooks; Becky Cheung; Heather Collins; Consumers Glass; Jane Crist; Cynthia Dahl; Matthew Dewar; Jim, Stephanie, Brian and Madeline Drake; Ruth and Charlie Drake; Cindy and Tom Drake; Liivi Georgievski; Wendy Le Grand; Linda Granfield; Bart Hall; Mryka and Ethan Hall-Beyer; Christine Hedden; Terry Horgan; Mandy Kan; Dr. John Kaufmann; Bob Lank; Sue Leppington; Ed Leslie; Claire Levy-Freedman; David, Melanie, Jennifer, and Adrian Love; Donna O'Connor; Neil Packham; Recycling Council of Canada; Wendy Reifel; Hilary Robinson; Mike Robson; George Sheridan; Kim Tanaka; Dr. and Mrs. Tashiro; Mary Thompson; Jane Tsui; Becky Worsley; Bernie Yeung; Keith Yoon.

It was a pleasure to renew editorial ties with Val Wyatt, whose phone calls, faxes and e-mails were punctuated with good humor, the occasional exclamation point and oxox! Thank you also to Valerie Hussey, Ricky Englander and the people at Kids Can Press.

We acknowledge the support of the Canada Council for the Arts and the Ontario Arts Council for our publishing program.

Canadian Cataloguing in Publication Data

Drake, Jane
    The kids guide to the millennium

Includes index.
ISBN 1-55074-556-5 (bound)
ISBN 1-55074-436-4 (pbk.)

1. Millennium – Juvenile literature. 2. Two thousand, A.D. – Juvenile literature. 3. Civilization – History – Juvenile literature. 4. Twenty-first century – Forecasts – Juvenile literature. I. Love, Ann . II. Slavin, Bill. III. Title.

CB429.D72 1998 j909 C97-931000-8

Text copyright © 1998 by Jane Drake and Ann Love
Illustrations copyright © 1998 by Bill Slavin

Many of the designations used by manufacturers and sellers to distinguish their products are claimed as trademarks. Where those designations appear in this book and Kids Can Press Ltd. was aware of a trademark claim, the designations have been printed in initial capital letters (e.g., Supercard).

Neither the Publisher nor the Author shall be liable for any damage which may be caused or sustained as a result of conducting any of the activities in this book without specifically following instructions, conducting the activities without proper supervision, or ignoring the cautions contained in the book.

Published in Canada by
Kids Can Press Ltd.
29 Birch Avenue
Toronto, ON M4V 1E2

Published in the U.S. by
Kids Can Press Ltd.
85 River Rock Drive, Suite 202
Buffalo, NY 14207

Edited by Valerie Wyatt
Designed by Marie Bartholomew and Esperança Melo

Printed and bound in Canada by Kromar Printing Limited.

CM 98 0 9 8 7 6 5 4 3 2 1
CM PA 98 0 9 8 7 6 5 4 3 2 1

CONTENTS

YOU'RE INVITED TO THE MILLENNIUM

Decades come every 10 years, centuries every 100, but a millennium comes around only once every 1000 years.

Earth's third millennium begins January 1, 2000. How can you celebrate? This book is packed with ideas that range from challenging and caring to weird and wacky. So come and join kids all around the world and celebrate the new millennium. As you go, follow the time line starting on page 5. A lot has happened in 2000 years!

You're invited to:
A New Millennium
Date: January 1, 2000
Place: Everywhere on the Planet!

Or is it the millennium?

Weeks, months and years — various people invented different parts of our calendar. The way we count years comes from early Christians. They used the letters A.D. to show years after Jesus' birthday and B.C. for years before. So 2000 A.D. means 2000 years after Jesus was born.

When people started counting years in this way, they didn't include a year 0 between 1 B.C. and 1 A.D. If they started counting at year 1, then 2000 years will not really have passed until the year 2001. Whoops — are we actually celebrating the millennium one year early?

TIME LINE

1 A.D.

World population reaches 170 million. Turn to page 63 to find out the population in the year 2000.

5
China

According to a legend, Ko Yu invents the wheelbarrow.

20
Rome

A new spice from India, pepper, becomes popular.

50
China

Cooks serve noodles for the first time.

50
Rome

Metal horseshoes, called hipposandals, are invented.

80
Rome

The Colosseum opens with chariot races and gladiator fights.

COUNTDOWN CALENDAR

Are you counting the days to January 1, 2000? Make a countdown calendar to help you pass the time.

1. Put the small cardboard square on one of the larger pieces of white cardboard and use the pencil to trace around three sides, as shown.

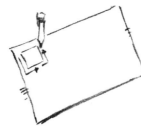

2. Ask an adult to help you cut around the three sides. Fold the flap back along the dotted line to make a little door.

3. Cut 11 more of these little doors.

4. Draw a picture on the cardboard. Color right over the doors.

5. Put the other sheet of cardboard under the one with doors. Use paper clips to hold it in place. Open all the doors and use a pencil to trace their outlines on the cardboard underneath.

6. Inside each square on the bottom card, draw a picture. You could draw 12 inventions from the past that you couldn't live without, or your 12 greatest hopes for the future, or anything else you wish.

7. Put glue around the edge of the bottom card on the same side as your drawings. Place the top card over the bottom card so the picture faces up.

8. Open one door on January 31, 1999, another door on the last day of February 1999, and so on. The last door will be ready to open on New Millennium Eve 1999.

100
China
Rudders are first used to help steer boats.

105
China
Tsai Lun makes writing paper out of water and rags.

110
Mexico
Chocolate becomes a popular drink.

132
China
The first earthquake detector successfully shows the direction of the epicenter (source) of an earthquake.

180
Rome
Galen writes a book on the human body, after a career of treating wounded gladiators.

200
Italy
Shoes are first made for left and right feet.

MILLENNOGRAMS

Pssssst! The new millennium is coming. Spread the word. Forget about snail mail or phone calls. Try these wild and crazy millennograms instead.

WILD!

What's round, brown, wrinkly and good at keeping a secret? A walnut with a message inside. Sound nuts to you? Try it and see.

YOU WILL NEED

walnuts

a nutcracker

a small fork

paper and a pen

white glue

1. Crack several walnuts in half with the nutcracker. It may take a couple of tries until you can crack one without shattering it.

2. Pick out the walnut meat with your fingers or a small fork.

3. Write a millennium greeting on a slip of paper and put it into an empty half shell.

4. Squeeze glue around the lip of the shell and put the other half shell on top to seal the nut back together. Hand out these millennium nuts and watch your friends go nuts.

WHAT TO SAY

What's the perfect millennogram message? Try these messages or make up your own.

* You're better looking every millennium!

* See you in the next millennium.

* May the new millennium bring you many good-hair days.

* Redeem this coupon for 2000 seconds of my time.
P.S. — I'm really yours for all time!

CRAZY!

If you have a computer hook-up that allows you to send e-mail, send your millennium greetings electronically. Just for fun, send your message in a code devised two millennia ago. To find out how, check out the Caesar code at the Classic Ciphers website (http://rschp2.anu.edu.au:8080/cipher.html). While you're there, translate this greeting: kdssb ploohqqlxp!

Add some smileys to your message. Smileys are e-mail punctuation marks that read sideways. They're meant to express emotions.

For example:
:-) means smile
:- D means laugh

Here's a millennial greeting full of smileys: My :-& and my :-X until we ^)^ ^(^ in 2000. If you can't translate it, click on your Internet search icon and look up "smileys."

A millennium ago, European monks invented the first smiley — the exclamation mark! At the end of an important sentence, the monks put a tiny "o" instead of a period and then placed an upside down "i" on top. This meant "oi" or "joy" in Greek. Use the exclamation mark as a millennial smiley in your millennograms!

200
Northern Europe
People tie animal shinbones under their boots and make the first ice skates.

247
Rome
The city is declared 1000 years old. Millennium celebrations are held.

256
Syria
Knitting and crocheting are used to make socks.

270
Rome
St. Valentine is sentenced to death for marrying young lovers against the Emperor's wishes.

285
Egypt
Machines with levers, screws, pulleys, wedges and cogwheels are used to make work easier.

THROW A NEW MILLENNIUM PARTY

If you think New Year's Eve is special, imagine a New Year that happens only once every thousand years. To celebrate, throw a party. A Very Special Party.

MMARVELOUS DECORATIONS

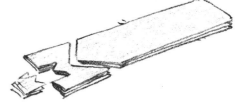

The Romans wrote the number 2000 as MM. Use the double M as your party theme. Start with some MM banners to drape around the party room.

YOU WILL NEED

a square of colored construction paper 18 cm x 18 cm (7 in. x 7 in.)

a pencil

scissors

clear tape

1. Fold the paper in half and in half again. Your paper should look like this:

2. Draw a capital M on the bottom of the folded paper. Cut it out.

3. Open up the cut-out M to form a chain of M's. Repeat and make more chains of M's. Tape lots of chains together and make a banner to drape over a doorway or across a room. Or decorate yourself. Cut a construction paper headband 5 cm (2 in.) wide. Tape M chains to the top of the headband and you've got your very own millennial crown.

NOISEMAKERS

Bells ring, horns blow and pots are banged to welcome the new year. Why all the racket? It was once thought that loud noises chased away evil and scared the devil out of the next year. To keep this tradition going into the next millennium, make this noisemaker.

YOU WILL NEED

5 cm (2 in.) of clear tape

10-15 streamers, metallic icicles or thin strips of tissue paper, each 15 cm (6 in.) long

a large straw

scissors

1. Lay the tape on a flat surface, sticky side up. Space the streamers evenly along the tape.

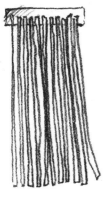

2. Wrap the tape around one end of the straw, so that the streamers hang off the end.

3. Flatten the other end of the straw and use scissors to snip off the corners. Place this end in your mouth and blow.

300
Turkey
Forks are used at the dinner table for the first time.

330
Central America
The Mayans are first to use a symbol for zero in their mathematical calculations.

350
India
The first hospitals for ordinary people are opened.

360
Europe
Books begin to take the place of scrolls.

393
Rome
Pants are banned — men must wear skirts.

395
Egypt
Hypatia is named the first woman teacher at the university in Alexandria.

PARTY FARE

New Millennium Eve isn't a night for hot dogs and paper plates. Step back in time and make some food that people ate 1000 or 2000 years ago.

A thousand years ago, the Maya and Aztec people of Central and South America ate foods that were unknown to the rest of the world. You can eat what they ate by stuffing corn tortillas with a mixture of cooked corn, hot and sweet peppers, squash, potatoes and tomatoes. Finish the meal with a chocolate dessert. A millennium ago, all of these foods (including chocolate) were only available in Central and South America.

Or step farther back in time and eat like a rich Roman did 2000 years ago. Dine on favorite Roman foods: grapes, olives, pickles, ham, oysters, pike, goat, wild asparagus, eggs, pears, apples and bread covered with poppy seeds. Hmmmm ... anyone for pike on poppy with a pickle?

WELCOME LIGHTS

Light the path to your millennium party with candles glowing in paper bags.

YOU WILL NEED

small brown, flat-bottomed paper bags

sand

candle stubs, at least 10 cm (4 in.) tall

matches

1. Fold over the top of each bag.

2. Moisten some sand with water and put 10 to 15 cm (4 to 6 in.) of sand in the bottom of each bag.

3. Place the bags along the path to your home. Anchor one candle stub securely in the sand in the middle of each bag and ask an adult to help you light the candles. The welcome lights will make a glowing path to your door. (The lights are reusable — just dampen the sand each time before using.)

4. Is the snow too deep for paper-bag candles? Poke a deep hole into a soft snowbank and wedge in a candle stub. Stick it in far enough so that the candle can't be seen from the outside. Carefully light the candle with a long-handled match. Presto — snow glow.

400
Mexico
The Mayans play a game like soccer, using knee and elbow pads and a hard rubber ball.

409
China
The umbrella is invented.

433
Germany
Attila becomes leader of the Huns. Under his leadership, the Huns conquer the center of Europe.

450
Peru
Tubas, drums, flutes and horns are used in music.

490
Burgundy (France)
A timepiece called a clepsydra uses dripping water to measure time.

2000 THINGS TO DO ON NEW MILLENNIUM EVE

Carry the 2000 theme to the extreme with these 2000 games. If you play them for 2000 seconds, you'll be 33.33 minutes closer to the year 2000.

WHAT'S HOT IN 2000?

Radio stations will calculate the top 2000 tunes of all time and magazines are voting on their Man or Woman of the Millennium. You too can grade the millennium — who and what is hot (or not). Think up the top ten for each of the following categories:

* musicians
* inventions
* bad guys
* good guys
* disasters
* explorers
* athletes
* movies

Compare your top ten with those of your friends and family.

ONE IN 2000

Transform some spare change into a 2000 game. Collect 2000 pennies. One should be dated 1999; the others any year before 1999. Spread out the pennies on a table.

Take turns to see who can find the 1999 penny fastest.

If your money's all in the bank, but you have a huge bottle cap collection, label one cap with a tiny MM and then play as

described before. You can play with anything — 2000 peanuts in the shell, 2000 puzzle pieces, 2000 buttons, 2000 marbles. Just mark one of the 2000 with the double M.

PACK YOUR BAG

What's your vision for the future? Plan for the new millennium by playing this game.

Sitting in a circle, the youngest player begins with "I packed my bag for the millennium and in it I put peace on Earth." The next youngest person says "I packed my bag for the millennium and in it I put peace on Earth and gummy worms." Continue adding to the bag until it is so full that you can't remember everything, or it has 2000 items, whichever comes first.

This game can also be played as "I packed my bag for the millennium and in it I *didn't* put": AIDS, bullies, chores, pollution, broccoli, grunge, homework ...

508
France
False beards are banned.

525
Rome
A calendar that starts numbering the years at Jesus' birth is introduced.

541
Turkey
The bubonic plague kills up to 10 000 people a day.

550
England
King Arthur (of Round Table fame) is killed.

570
Arabia
The prophet Mohammed is born in Mecca.

589
Turkey
The Empress Theodora, a powerful force in government, dies.

MILLENNIAL MINIGLOBE

Make a miniglobe for your bedroom and follow the millennium as it dawns around the world.

YOU WILL NEED

a large round balloon

newspaper

flour-and-water paste

a world atlas

paints

paintbrush

1 m (3 ft.) of strong string

2. Tear the newspaper into strips 5 cm (2 in.) long. Dip the strips into the flour-and-water paste and remove any extra. Cover the balloon completely with a layer of paper strips as shown.

4. Using a world atlas as a guide, paint the main land and water forms. Draw in the international date line. Draw a star where you live.

1. Blow up the balloon. Tie the neck. This will be the north pole of your globe.

3. Add a second layer of newspaper strips, then allow the globe to dry.

5. Tie the string to the neck of your miniglobe and hang it up.

Following the millennium

If you want to be the first person on Earth to see the dawning of the new millennium, head for the international date line. The date line is an imaginary line that goes from the north pole to the south pole through the Pacific Ocean. East of the date line is one day, west of it is the next day.

The millennium will happen first all along the date line. But the very first *dry land* to see *sunrise* on January 1, 2000, will be the Pacific islands of Tonga, Wallis Island, Fiji and Tuvalu. They get to be first because they're near the Tropic of Capricorn, the part of Earth tilted closest to the sun. More northerly places along the date line will still be in darkness.

The new millennium will progress westward around the globe, with New Zealand welcoming in 2000 before Australia, Japan, China, India, and so on, as the world turns. Finally, it will dawn January 1 on the westernmost Hawaiian islands.

Where will you be when the world turns 2000? Check the time zones of the world and calculate what time it will be where you live when the sun rises over the date line in the Pacific and the new millennium dawns.

600
India
The game of chess is invented.

600
Central America
The Mayans make false teeth from seashells.

607
Japan
The Hōryū-ji temple and hospital are built of wood. They still stand today.

609
India
The decimal point is first used in math.

651
Arabia
The Koran, the sacred book of the Islamic people, is written.

674
England
The first glass windows are made.

WESTWARD LETTER

Make new pen-pals by sending a millennium greeting to kids around the world. Mail a short letter to someone who lives west of you. Ask that person to add to the letter and mail it to a friend living still farther west. After zigzagging westward around the world, the letter should end up back in your mailbox.

January 1, 2000
221 Creek Dr.
North Tickle, Newfoundland
Canada A2A 1A1

Hi Sam,
To celebrate the year 2000, I am sending a letter westward — the direction in which time travels. Please say hello in the way you do where you live, and add some information about yourself. Then send this letter to someone who lives west of you. Let's see if we can send the letter all the way around the world during the millennium year. The person who has the letter on December 31, 2000, should mail it back to me.
Where I come from it's cool to say "Hey, What's up?" I'm 12 and I love to play soccer.
Happy Millennium,

Stephanie Smith

Include the date and your complete address.

Say "hi" the way you would greet a friend where you live.

Briefly explain why you are sending the letter. Tell the recipient to add his name, address and message and send the letter westward.

Include some information about yourself.

18

Letter-writing tips

* Use simple language — your letter may have to be translated.

* Include a photo of yourself, if you wish.

* When the letter returns to you, make photocopies and mail them to all the contributors, so that they can see where the letter has traveled.

November 2, 2000
10 Hibiscus Street
Toowoomba, Queensland 4352
Australia

G'day Brian,
We're planning a trip to Maroochydore for the summer hols — and a millennium party on the beach! I'm packing my snorkel and mask. Hope the jellyfish don't sting!
Hooray,

Pete

700
Europe
Eggs are first used in the celebration of Easter.

711
Spain
The lute and an early violin, invented by Arabs, are introduced to Europe.

748
China
The first newspaper is printed.

778
England
A silver coin is minted and named the penny.

789
France
King Charlemagne uses his foot as a unit of length. The foot is still used today in the United States and some other countries.

791
Morocco
The leader, Iman Idris, is killed with a poisoned toothpick.

JANUARY 1, 2000: DEAR DIARY

Imagine if a future historian came across your diary. She could learn a lot about your world from what you wrote. Of course, in order for that to happen, you have to write the diary in the first place. Why not start a diary on the first day of the new millennium. To get you going, try these tips:

* Choose a regular time to write, such as before bed or after dinner. Try to write at least three times a week.

* For privacy, use a diary that has a lock or hide your diary. Use code words to baffle spies.

* Give your diary a name — you'll feel you are writing to a person.

* Write about things that interest you. If you like movies, write about them.

* Write about your feelings. In the future, you'll want to know what you felt as well as what happened.

PAST DIARIES

Old diaries, journals and chronicles tell a lot about life in the past. A millennium ago, monks in England kept a record of major events. In the year 995, their Anglo-Saxon Chronicle recorded the appearance of a "long-haired star." The monks had seen a comet.

Three hundred years later, Marco Polo traveled to China. Through his trip diaries, Europeans learned about the Chinese use of paper money, fire-fighters, coal, the compass and many other inventions.

Future diaries

What will the world be like on December 31, 2999? Record your ideas in a diary entry.

December 31, 2999

Dear Diary:

Today, on our way to Zargol's New Millennium party, we flew past the Butterfly Spaceship dock. It was resting after the Andromeda circuit. We couldn't fly too close in case it moved one of its huge wings in its sleep. It has been having muscle spasms after hitting an intergalactic dust storm on the return trip. We saw the chrysalis of another one almost ready to hatch. Mum said we have intergalactic travel now because people a millennium ago decided to protect wildlife, including butterflies. There's no way machines could have taken us so far.

800
Scandinavia
The Vikings build longboats that can carry 30 warriors in heavy seas.

802
Europe
The first rose bushes are planted.

840
Spain
The first public hairdressing and beauty salon opens.

850
China
Warnings are issued not to make a dangerous new invention, gunpowder.

868
China
A book called *Diamond Sutra* is printed. It is the oldest printed book that still exists.

885
France
The Vikings sail up the Seine River and invade Paris.

ME AT THE MILLENNIUM

"Hey! It's my birthday, too!" Make your birthday in the year 2000 super special by preserving a record of yourself. Here are some things to collect.

On your birthday 10 or 20 years from now, open up your personal time capsule and see how you have changed — and how you have stayed the same.

* A photo taken on your birthday in the year 2000. Write your height and weight on the back.

* Your birthday party invitation

* News headlines or TV listings from your millennial birthday

* A recent movie, sports or concert ticket stub

* A family or sports photo

* Your footprint

* A clipping of your hair

* A favorite piece of clothing

EXPRESS

* Place all items in a plastic bag, press out the air and seal with tape.

* Put the bag in a metal or plastic container with a tight-fitting lid to protect it.

Ancient time capsules

A time capsule preserves objects from here and now for the unknown future. Archaeologists like to find ancient time capsules because they tell a lot about life long ago.

The Egyptian pyramids are time capsules. More than 4000 years ago, Egyptian pharaohs constructed these huge tombs to seal in themselves and their possessions forever. Today, archaeologists use the treasures and everyday objects found in pyramids to untangle the true story of ancient Egypt.

Sometimes archaeologists find accidental time capsules. The town of Pompeii, in Italy, was buried in volcanic ash when Mount Vesuvius erupted nearly 2 millennia ago. Archaeologists have dug out the town and pieced together a detailed story of life back then from this gruesome, natural time capsule.

900
Iraq
The first theme park is built. It has mechanical statues of singing birds and roaring lions.

929
Germany
Good King Wenceslas is murdered by his brother.

950
Iraq and Iran
Stories from *The Thousand and One Arabian Nights*, including "Aladdin" and "Ali Baba," are popular.

975
Europe
Mathematicians write numerals as 1, 2, 3, 4, instead of I, II, III, IV.

999
Europe
Some people are so sure the world will end in the year 1000 that they do not plant crops for next year's food.

MY FAMILY AT THE MILLENNIUM

A photograph shows what your family looks like, but a patchwork quilt can record how your family lived. Dad's weekend shirt, brother's soccer jersey and Gran's housecoat can be made into a wall hanging that will keep memories alive well into the next millennium.

YOU WILL NEED

a piece of cardboard 11 cm x 11 cm (4½ in. x 4½ in.)

a clean piece of clothing from everyone in your family. (Ask permission first; the clothing will be cut apart. Cotton fabric works best.)

a fine-tipped marker

sharp scissors

straight pins

needle and thread

thin quilt padding 30 cm x 30 cm (12 in. x 12 in.)

plain fabric

white chalk

seam binding

a wooden dowel or straight twig at least 35 cm (14 in.) long

1. Place the cardboard square on a piece of family clothing. (Doublecheck that the clothing is no longer wanted.) Draw around it with a fine-tipped marker. Cut out the fabric square. Cut out nine squares in all, each

2. Pin two squares together, wrong sides out. Sew a seam 5 mm (¼ in.) along one edge.

3. Pin a third square to make a row of three squares. Sew a seam 5 mm (¼ in.) along the connecting edge.

4. Repeat to make two more rows.

5. With right sides together, pin and sew the top and middle rows together. Repeat for the middle and bottom rows. Iron the seams flat.

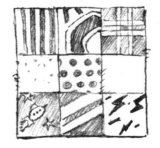

6. Make a sandwich that looks like this. Sew around the square, as close to the outside edge as possible.

fabric (right side up)

quilt batting   **plain fabric**

7. Use the chalk to draw a design on the patchwork square. Sew along the chalk lines with small, neat stitches. Sew through all three layers of fabric.

8. Sew the seam binding around the edge of the square.

9. Sew two seam binding loops onto one edge of the square. Put the dowel or twig through the loops and hang your patchwork wall hanging on a wall.

Ancient art

Quilts have been found buried in Egyptian tombs that date back to 3400 B.C. Over the centuries, quilts have been used for warmth, decoration and even to thicken knights' armor.

1000

World population reaches 265 million people.

1000

Canada

Explorer Leif Ericsson lands in Newfoundland.

1021

Europe

An epidemic of St. Vitus's dance sweeps Europe. Some people lose all control of their muscles and flail their arms and legs and make wild faces.

1026

Italy

Musician Guido d'Arezzo teaches singing using "ut, re, mi, fa, sol, la." Now we sing "do, re, mi, fa, so, la, ti, do."

1041

China

A new printing method that uses individual letters rather than whole words makes printing easier and faster. It is called "movable type."

DESIGN A MILLENNIUM T-SHIRT

YOU WILL NEED

250 mL (1 c.) flour in a clean plastic squeeze bottle with a lid (such as an empty shampoo bottle)

150 mL (2/3 c.) water

newspaper

a clean, plain T-shirt

a crayon

permanent fabric paint (must be thick, not runny)

a paintbrush

a clean cloth

an iron

What would a major event be without a T-shirt to commemorate it? But what to put on a new millennium T-shirt? You need a symbol. Symbols say something without using words. Toddlers know what they'll get under the Golden Arches. And a stop sign means stop all over the world. Show people what the new millennium means to you by creating a symbol. Then batik your symbol onto a T-shirt. Traditional batik uses hot wax and dye. Here's a cool (and less messy) alternative.

1. Slowly add the water to the flour in the bottle. Pour in a bit at a time and mix by shaking the bottle. The paste should be the consistency of porridge. Put the lid on the bottle.

2. Cover your work area with newspaper and smooth the T-shirt on top.

3. Use a crayon to draw your symbol onto the fabric. Define the outside edge of the symbol with a border.

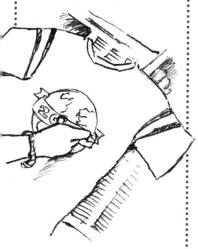

4. Gently squeeze a thin line of flour-and-water paste along the lines you have drawn for the border. Squeeze lines of paste along the rest of the lines that make up the design. Allow to dry completely.

5. Paint over the design. Keep inside the border, but cover all the paste. When the paint is dry, pick off the paste to reveal your symbol.

6. Cover the symbol with a clean cloth and iron to set the paint.

WILD SYMBOLS

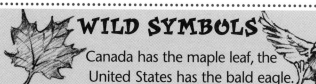

Canada has the maple leaf, the United States has the bald eagle. What wildlife symbol would be good for the millennium? Termites and fish can lay 2000 eggs, bristlecone pines live over 2000 years. Can you think of other 2000 tie-ins?

1050
China
The first fireworks are set off.

1065
Europe
Wealthy men learn horsemanship and chivalry at knight school.

1090
Italy
Trotula, a famous female doctor, believes prevention, not surgery, cures her patients.

1094
Italy
Gondolas are first used on the canals of Venice.

1099
Palestine
The city of Jerusalem is sacked by Christian crusaders, and all inhabitants are slaughtered.

1100
Europe
Chimneys are built into homes for the first time.

SET A MILLENNIUM RECORD

Youth Skips into the Next Millennium

What better time to attempt the impossible than the new millennium? Why not set a personal millennial goal and go for it? Use the event to raise money for a good cause. Call the local paper and tell them that you plan to set a new record — you might make headlines!

Kids Swim into New Year: $ Raised for Wilderness

KAMLOOPS. Our local swim club crawled into the new millennium with a tag team swim-a-thon that netted $4800 for wilderness preservation. Coach and record keeper Ian Barnett proudly told of club members' determination to stay afloat until midnight. "The original plan was to swim the distance around the globe, but we modified that to a team challenge of 2000 lengths. The kids were sponsored on a per-length basis. Each team member swam five lengths, high-fived the next swimmer and rested." Waterlogged but happy, swim club members dug into a midnight feast before wishing each other Happy New Millennium.

CHICAGO. Ten-year-old Jackie Lee skipped her way through the millennium without missing a step. She began skipping at 11:30 P.M. and was skipping her 2000th skip when the clock tolled the new millennium. Puffing for breath, Jackie described her accomplishment: "I trained hard for this event. I love skipping, and I thought it would be a fun and fit way to celebrate the arrival of the new millennium." Her brother, when asked why he wasn't skipping, declared, "I'm waiting for the summer so I can canoe for a thousand hours." He will need a long vacation to achieve that goal!

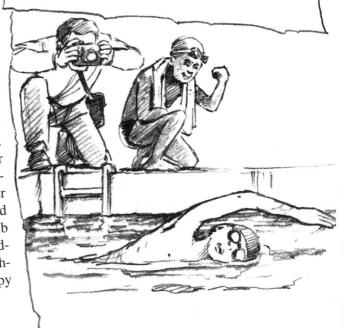

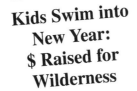

Crazy challenges

People attempt the wildest feats. For the record, would you eat 50 ears of corn or learn to play the harmonica with your nose? If the idea of growing a millennial fingernail gets clipped, organize an event that capitalizes on your special talents or interests: a hockey slapshot challenge, a somersault-a-thon, a marathon chess tournament. Need some inspiration? According to *The Guinness Book of World Records*, 14 students from Hanover High School in New Hampshire leap-frogged 1429.2 km (888.1 mi.) in record time — 189 hours and 49 minutes. Do you think you could make it 2000 km (1242 mi.)?

1100
Europe
Advances in stained-glass technology make color windows possible.

1100
England
The first university in England is founded at Oxford.

1107
China
Money is printed in color, making counterfeiting tougher.

1139
Nigeria
An Igbo leader dies and is buried with elegant bronze sculptures made by local metal workers.

1140
France
Doctors must have a license to practice medicine.

1147
Russia
The city of Moscow is established.

SEND A FOSSIL TO THE FUTURE

YOU WILL NEED

a large plastic soft-drink bottle

a craft knife

a soup spoon

powdered plaster of paris

items that say something about you (nail clippings, hair trimmings, a baby tooth, a fur ball from your cat, and so on)

The millennium means that the Earth is turning 2000, right? Wrong. Earth is actually 4½ billion years old — give or take a few hundred millennia. Living things have been around for 570 million of those years. Scientists know when and where creatures lived by studying fossils, the petrified (turned-to-rock) remains of long-dead plants and animals. You can turn bits of yourself into a soft-drink-bottle fossil to mark your place in history.

1. Ask an adult to help you cut the top off a plastic soft-drink bottle with the craft knife.

2. Spoon about 3 cm (1 in.) of plaster of paris into the bottom of the bottle. Drop in your first item. Cover it with a spoonful of plaster of paris. Continue until you have buried everything, ending with a layer of plaster 3 cm (1 in.) deep.

3. Slowly pour water into the bottle. Tap and squeeze the sides to allow it to flow to the bottom. Fill the bottle with enough water to cover the top layer of plaster.

Radiocarbon dating

Fossils are clocks.
How do scientists tell their time?

By using a process called radiocarbon dating. This process tells the age of anything that was once alive or that contains traces of carbon, such as paper, hair, teeth or bananas. If you want your fossil to reveal something about you to a future scientist, preserve only organic (living or once-living) objects.

BEST BEFORE 2000 A.D.

ROCK OF AGES

If you find a rock that looks like it's made up of layers, then you may be holding a sedimentary rock. Sedimentary rocks formed when layers of sand and debris collected on the bottom of shallow seas. Over thousands of years, the bottom layers were crushed into stone by the layers on top. Each layer may be millennia older than the one above it.

4. Allow to dry for several days. Ask an adult to help you cut away the plastic bottle to reveal your fossil. Won't it boggle future scientists?

1150
France
An early form of tennis is first played.

1151
China
Explosives, rockets and tear gas are used in warfare.

1174
Italy
A magnificent tower is built in Pisa — it later leans.

1179
Central America
The Mayapan people destroy the famous Mayan city of Chichén Itzá, driving the few survivors into the wilderness.

1200
Europe
Buttons are first used on clothing.

1200
Mexico
Chewing gum becomes popular.

MARKING TIME

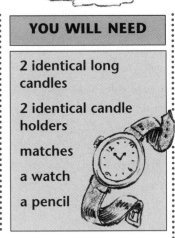

How good are you at guessing the time? People long ago realized everyone has a slightly different sense of time. They needed units of time that everyone could agree on — like hours, minutes and seconds.

A millennium ago, kings and queens lit candle clocks to tell the hours. Here's how to turn a candle into a clock.

YOU WILL NEED

2 identical long candles

2 identical candle holders

matches

a watch

a pencil

1. Put the two candles in the candle holders. Be sure they are straight and the same height.

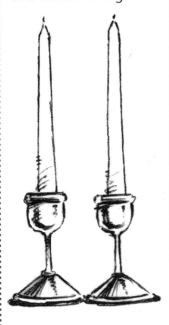

2. Ask an adult to help light one candle. After one hour, blow out the flame. Use the pencil point to mark the height of the burned candle on the side of the unburned candle.

3. Relight the partially burned candle and wait for another hour. Mark that height on the unburned candle. Repeat until there is nothing left of the burning candle. The remaining candle can now be used as a clock. When it burns to the one-hour mark, you'll know one hour has passed. Can you mark half and quarter hours on your candle clock, too?

It's a date

How did people keep track of the days before calendars were invented?

* Long ago people used the moon to mark the passing days. They called the time from one new moon to the next a "moonth." Sound familiar? The trouble is that moon cycles don't coincide with the seasons, so it's hard to predict dates like harvest using the moon alone.

* Five millennia ago, Thoth, an Egyptian, invented a sun calendar. He divided the year into 12 months, each 30 days long. That left some extra days for a holiday at year's end.

* Four millennia ago, people in Iraq divided the days into hours, minutes and seconds. They also grouped days into weeks — seven days between markets.

* About two millennia ago, Julius Caesar eliminated the New Year's holiday and added the extra days to different months. That's why some months have more days than others. The Romans gave the months their names. July was named after Julius himself.

* Over the years the dates and seasons slipped apart because the sun year is not quite 365¼ days. To catch up, Pope Gregory in 1582 declared that October 4 would be followed by October 15. We still use his "Gregorian calendar" today.

1200
Europe
Engagement rings are used for the first time.

1201
Mediterranean Sea
A catastrophic earthquake in the area kills 1 million people.

1202
Europe
Court jesters are first employed by royalty.

1204
France
Eleanor, Queen of France and later England, dies after reigning for more than 50 years.

1212
Germany and France
Thousands of children join in a crusade to the Holy Land. Most are sold as slaves, starve to death or drown.

1218
Asia
Mongol ruler Ghenghis Khan conquers and rules lands across Asia from China to eastern Europe.

BIG TIME

Earth's rocky crust formed about 3.7 million millennia ago (that's about 3.7 billion years). Europe and North America split apart 180 000 millennia ago, forming the Atlantic Ocean. And the Himalaya Mountains rose 50 000 millennia ago. In all, Earth's geological history spans more than 4.5 million millennia — that's big time.

Human history is shorter, but still longer than you might think. Make your own time line to find out what humans have been up to.

YOU WILL NEED

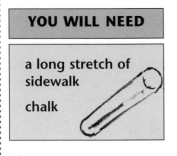

a long stretch of sidewalk

chalk

1. Mark one end of the sidewalk with a chalk line and write the word TODAY.

2. Stand with your toes just touching the line and take one pace forward. (A pace is made by taking one natural step.) Label where your toe lands 1000 A.D.

3. Take another pace and mark the year 1 A.D. The next pace is 1000 B.C., then 2000 B.C., 3000 B.C., and so on. With each pace, you step another 1000 years back in time. Keep taking and marking paces until you come to 200 000 B.C. (200 paces).

4. Here are some important dates in human history to find on your time line:

1000 B.C. Use of our alphabet started to spread.

2000 B.C. An early kind of plow was invented.

3000 B.C. Wheels and carts were first used in transportation.

6000 B.C. Cloth was first woven.

7000 B.C. Chickens were first domesticated.

10 000 B.C. Houses were first built with sun-dried bricks.

20 000 B.C. The bow and arrow were invented.

30 000 B.C. People first wore beads, bracelets and necklaces.

50 000 B.C. Humans started to bury their dead with ceremony.

80 000 B.C. Earliest stone lamps were used.

200 000 B.C. Stone hammers were first used to shape stone axes.

RULES OF THUMB

Ancient measurements were based on body parts because they were, well, handy. The "pace" is one ancient unit of measure. Other ancient units include:

* the "digit" or width of a finger

* the "palm" or width of four fingers

* the "cubit" or the distance between the elbow and the end of the middle finger

* the "fathom" or the distance between outstretched arms

Although these "rules of thumb" are not absolutely accurate, they enabled ancient builders to construct such monuments as the Pyramid of Cheops, which has stood for more than four millennia!

1250
Europe
The goose feather quill is first used as a pen for writing.

1260
Europe
Written musical notes start to show how long a sound is held.

1262
North America
After a severe drought, the Mesa Verde cliff dwellings are abandoned.

1271
China
Marco Polo, from Italy, arrives in China to trade. He meets Emperor Kublai Khan and learns about important Chinese inventions such as paper money and the compass.

1280
Germany
The spinning wheel is invented.

1290
South America
Rope cable bridges are built across mountain canyons to connect villages.

A DAY IN THE LIFE

"So, how was your day?" "I slept in, teased my brother, ate on the bus, went to school, had peanut butter for lunch, played soccer, came home, walked the dog, munched a snack, watched TV, inhaled dinner, talked on the phone, did homework, fell asleep."

You have a full, busy life.

What would your life be like if you could travel back through the millennia — or forward?

A kid's life 1 A.D.

School: Rich boys go to school. Rich girls stay home, make pottery or embroider.

Food: Grapes, olives and grains

Sleeping: Large extended family and servants live under one roof. Luckily soap has been invented.

Fun: Gladiator fights, wrestling and gymnastics

Chores: All poor children work like slaves from sunup to sundown in fields, homes, streets. Some pick lice out of rich men's hair.

Family life: Men rule the family, punishing or even killing disobedient wives and children.

Worries: Being thrown to the lions

A kid's life 1000 A.D.

School: Priests teach wealthy boys. Girls learn at home until they marry, at about age ten.

Food: Most people dine on fruit and porridge, with milk and honey if they have money. Meat is reserved for lords and ladies.

Sleeping: Families sleep three or more to a bedroom, along with a cow or goat.

Fun: Watching a jousting tournament or crusaders marching past.

Chores: Hard work in field and forest kills most people by the time they're 30.

Family life: Crowded, smoky homes (chimneys aren't invented yet). Parents can't wait to sell or marry off their kids.

Worries: Viking invaders, natural disasters, getting the bubonic plague, the end of the world.

A kid's life 3000 A.D.

School: Learning at home over the Internet. No classrooms.

Food: Nutrition in a pill.

Sleeping: Four hours max in your total relaxation suspended sleep machine.

Fun: Looking through old books, such as *The Kids Guide to the Millennium*, and laughing at the predictions.

Chores: Robots do all the housework. You just issue commands.

Family life: Take your pick of solo life on a space module or live commune-style with other members of the galaxy.

Worries: What's your guess?

1314
Europe
"Mob soccer" is banned in the streets.

1325
Italy
The War of the Oaken Bucket kills thousands over the theft of an oak cask.

1329
Mexico
The Aztecs start building the city of Tenochtitlán (now Mexico City) at the place where an eagle, with a snake in its mouth, is seen sitting on a cactus.

1340
Belgium
The first blast furnace is developed near Liège. Its high temperatures allow stronger metal tools to be forged.

1340
Europe
People start to wear linen underwear, and personal hygiene improves.

1347-51
Europe
About 75 million Europeans die of the bubonic plague.

TIME WARP

Languages are like plants — they are alive and growing. Some words die off, while others take root and flourish. If you could travel back in time, you might be surprised to hear some expressions you use today. For example, do you recognize any of these sayings? All have survived for more than two millennia.

Leave no stone unturned.

Waste not fresh tears over old griefs.

There is always someone worse off than yourself.

Don't count your chickens before they are hatched.

Euripides (born 485 B.C., died 406 B.C.)

Aesop (born ?, died 550 B.C.)

Love conquers all.

The very hair on my head stand up for dread.

None loves the messenger who brings bad news.

Virgil (born 70 B.C., died 19 B.C.)

Sophocles (born 495 B.C., died 406 B.C.)

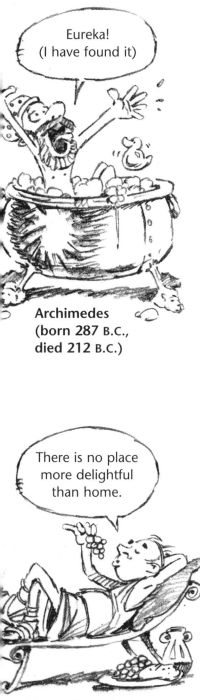

Eureka!
(I have found it)

Archimedes
(born 287 B.C.,
died 212 B.C.)

There is no place more delightful than home.

Cicero (born 106 B.C.,
died 43 B.C.)

New Year's expressions

People have been celebrating the new year longer than any other holiday. These old sayings come from New Year's Eve customs.

Scapegoat: In ancient times, a Jewish high priest laid his hands on the head of a goat, transferring all the evil from the people into the animal. The goat was sent off into the wilderness to take away bad luck for the new year.

Clean slate: Englishwomen believed that cleaning the slates on the roof would bring a year of good luck.

1350
Japan
The Shogun (ruler) bans the drinking of tea.

1369
France
Paris's famous prison, the Bastille, is built.

1390
Netherlands
Ice skating becomes popular.

1397
Italy
A new map is made showing Asia close to Europe. This map later inspires Christopher Columbus to sail west to find Asia, in 1492.

1400
Italy
Surgery is performed to replace cut-off noses using an ancient Hindu procedure.

1400
Europe
Men start wearing hose (tights) on their legs.

OLD WITHOUT MOLD

Did you eat a sandwich for lunch? If so, you were eating a food that's more than four millennia old. The sandwich was popular with ancient Egyptians when the pyramids were built.

(It didn't get the name sandwich until about 1700, when the Earl of Sandwich was busy playing cards and ordered his servants to fetch some meat between two pieces of bread.) The ancient Egyptians didn't use bread for their sandwiches; they used flatbreads similar to our modern pita. So grab a pita and make a 4000-year-old sandwich.

YOU WILL NEED

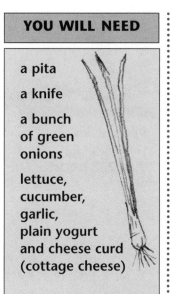

a pita

a knife

a bunch of green onions

lettuce, cucumber, garlic, plain yogurt and cheese curd (cottage cheese)

1. Cut the pita in half to make two sandwich pockets.

2. Chop the roots and green leaves off the onions. Slice the rest of the onion thinly and stuff into a pita pocket. Sweet onion was the favorite filling for ancient pitas.

3. Add your choice of the other fillings listed above. All of them were eaten by the workers who built the pyramids.

Eat your plate!

By 1000 A.D., people ate their meals on slices of stale bread called trenchers, and then ate the plate, too. Leftover trenchers were shared with servants, poor people and dogs. If you're having stew, put it on bread and eat it trencher-style.

BREAD AND BACTERIA

People usually throw out moldy bread, but the ancient Egyptians had a better idea. They pressed it onto wounds to help healing. In 1928, Dr. Alexander Fleming was studying a dangerous bacteria in his lab. By accident, his specimen was exposed to mold. He noticed the bacteria wouldn't grow where the mold did. He had discovered penicillin — a drug that fights bacterial infections.

1400
Belgium
Artists first use oil paint instead of egg tempera (a mixture of egg and coloring). Oil paints don't crack as much as egg tempera.

1402
Turkey
Tamerlane of Samarkand defeats the Sultan of Turkey. He makes a pyramid of lopped-off human heads and forces the Sultan to be his footstool.

1416
Netherlands
Drift nets are first used for fishing.

1431
France
Joan of Arc, once leader of the French army, is burned at the stake as a witch by the English.

1434
Portugal
Sailors travel south, along the coast of Africa, and discover that the southern seas are not full of monsters and boiling water as had been thought.

1448
Germany
Johannes Gutenberg re-invents the printing press and movable type. (See 1041 for its original invention.)

WHAT'S IT WORTH?

Archaeologists who dig into the lives of ancient people rejoice when they find a coin. A coin can contain vital facts such as the date and who ruled the land, information about trade, travel and farming, even the gods worshipped. Not exactly a microchip, but a coin packs a lot of info into a small disk.

To mark the millennium, preserve a set of coins from the year 2000. Your collection will make a great keepsake. Who knows — it might even be valuable in the future.

YOU WILL NEED

a box with a plastic lid (a notepaper box works well)

2 sets of coins minted in 2000

heavy cardboard cut to fit the interior of the box

a piece of felt larger than the cardboard

a pencil

a craft knife

white glue

1. Arrange one set of coins on the cardboard. Trace around each coin. Trace another identical row under the first.

2. With the help of an adult, use the craft knife to cut along the coin outlines.

3. Place the felt over the cardboard and press the coins into their proper holes. Trim the felt to the size of the cardboard and glue it down.

Heads

Tails

4. Put your coin collection into the box, cover it with the plastic lid and store in a safe place. If you are making a time capsule (page 22), add your collection to it.

Funny money

Birds' scalps, dogs' teeth, seashells, feathers, fish hooks, bricks of compressed tea and even cattle have been used as cash over the millennia. Here's some other "funny money."

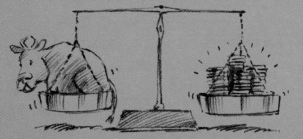

* A "buck" (a deer's skin) was used as money in China nearly two millennia ago.

* Ever heard the expression "earn some dough"? Roman soldiers were sometimes paid in bread dough.

* In 1887 an American named Edward Bellamy predicted that by the year 2000 people would no longer need money. Everyone would have government-issued cards stamped with each purchase.

* The Supercard is the latest in credit cards. It has a built-in computer that stores all your personal information. Use it to buy a CD or find out when your next allergy shot is due.

1450
Germany
The first eyeglasses are made for nearsighted people.

1477
Transylvania
Vlad IV, known as Dracula, dies in battle. His cruelty to prisoners leads to the legend of Count Dracula.

1485
England
The collected stories of King Arthur are printed.

1493
Caribbean
Christopher Columbus collects tobacco plants to take back to Spain.

1497
Canada
John Cabot reaches the east coast of Canada and claims the new land for England.

1500
China
Wan Hu dies while testing a flying machine made by attaching gunpowder rockets to a chair.

THE GAMES PEOPLE PLAY

You've got 26 000 points. Suddenly, one wrong move on the keypad and you're finished. "Game Over" blinks on the screen.

Tired of being outwitted by electronic wizardry? Try playing knucklebones, a game that has been around for more than two millennia. No batteries are required — just a small ball and five cleaned, dried bones (or fruit pits).

GETTING STARTED

To see who goes first, throw all five bones into the air and catch as many as possible on the back of your hand. Then toss the bones you caught and try to catch them in your palm. The person with the most bones goes first. She tries Ones. If she does it, she goes on to Twos, Threes, Fours and Fives and finally to Crack the Egg. Her turn is over when she fails to complete a trick. The player who completes the most tricks is the winner.

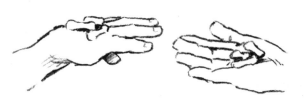

ONES

Throw the bones on the ground. Toss the ball into the air, pick up one bone and catch the ball after the first bounce. Use only one hand for both picking up the bones and catching the ball. Transfer the bone to the other hand and repeat until you have picked up all five bones.

TWOS, THREES, FOURS AND FIVES

Pick up two bones at a time, then three at a time, and so on, until you can pick up all five bones at once.

CRACK THE EGG

Throw the bones on the ground. Toss the ball in the air, pick up one bone, tap it on the ground (cracking the egg) and catch the ball after the first bounce. Continue until all five are picked up. Now play Twos, Threes, Fours and Fives, tapping the bones twice, three times, and so on. Did you drop any bones? If so, you're out.

GAME PIECES

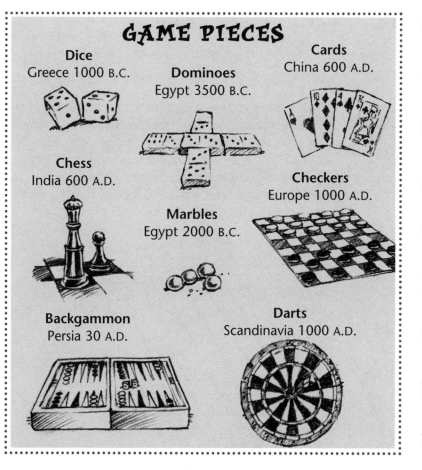

Dice
Greece 1000 B.C.

Dominoes
Egypt 3500 B.C.

Cards
China 600 A.D.

Chess
India 600 A.D.

Marbles
Egypt 2000 B.C.

Checkers
Europe 1000 A.D.

Backgammon
Persia 30 A.D.

Darts
Scandinavia 1000 A.D.

1500
England
The black-lead pencil is invented.

1503
Europe
Noses are wiped with the first handkerchiefs.

1508
Italy
Michelangelo starts painting the ceiling of the Sistine Chapel.

1512
Italy
Michelangelo finishes painting the ceiling of the Sistine Chapel.

1520
England
Henry VIII builds his own bowling alley.

1520
Spain
Chocolate from Mexico is first tasted in Europe.

1534-35
Canada
Jacques Cartier discovers Labrador and travels down the St. Lawrence River to Quebec and Montreal.

MILLENNIAL MUSIC

What music did people listen to one or two millennia ago? Some old instruments have survived, as have pictures of people playing them. So we can guess what sounds were possible.

One old instrument was pan pipes, made at least three millennia ago in ancient China, Peru and Greece. The originals were made from tough, hollow reeds such as bamboo, but you can make pan pipes from straws. Play them and you can hear sounds from millennia past.

1. Tape around the straws as shown.

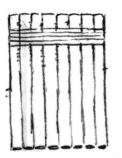

2. Touch the tops of the straws against your bottom lip. Blow straight across the top of the straws, not down into them. Can you hear a deep, whistle-like sound?

3. Now, tune your pan pipes. Starting at the left side, pinch the first straw near the bottom and blow across the top. Adjust your pinch point until you make a clear, low note. Cut the straw just below the pinch point and plug the bottom with modeling clay. Repeat with the remaining straws, making each one shorter until you have a full scale of notes.

The beat goes on

Have you sung a song
that is two millennia old?
You have if you've sung:

I'm the king of the castle
And you're the dirty rascal.

Similar words were sung in Rome in 20 B.C.
No one knows what tune went with them, but it
was probably similar to the one you sing today.

4. What tunes can you play with your pan pipes?

1553
Switzerland
Michael Servetus, who first described how the blood circulates in the human body, is burned at the stake for his religious beliefs.

1572
Netherlands
Pigeons are used to carry messages in a war with Spain.

1580
Europe
Pockets are first sewn in men's pants.

1589
France
Royalty start to use forks for dining.

1596
England
The first flush toilet is installed in the Queen's palace. (She doesn't use it because it's too scary and noisy.)

1600
England
William Shakespeare has written 20 plays to date.

GARBAGE TELLS A STORY

The family pet?

A hand-held television?

Post-exercise power juice?

Ear cleaner?

Imagine that it's several millennia from now. A spaceship hovers over Earth and gently touches down. The intergalactic visitors discover a landfill site, an exciting find. They begin to investigate. What does our garbage tell about us?

You can tell a lot about a civilization by what it has left behind. Four millennia ago, the people of Troy threw unwanted food and broken household pots onto the floor. When the mess became foul, they simply spread a layer of clay over the garbage. After a hundred years or so, the floor in a home could be as much as 1.5 m (4.6 ft.) higher, and a new ceiling and door frames had to be built. The layers of garbage sealed in by the clay provide a record of how the people lived back then.

What tales will our garbage tell future generations? No one knows for sure. But we do know that there will be a lot to look through. The average North American bags 1.8 kg (4 lb.) of garbage every day. Over a year, that adds up to enough steel to make a refrigerator, enough food for 300 meals and enough glass to make one bottle for every one thrown out. This trash ends up in the landfill site, never to be seen again.

Or that's what people think. In fact, garbologists (people who study landfills) say that garbage doesn't disappear — it gets squished into layers, just like in a home in Troy. Each layer preserves a compact history of the time, with the exact date of the layer recorded on tossed-out newspapers. Digging down in dumps, garbologists have found well-preserved

A damaged satellite?

A doorknob polisher?

Diet food?

hot dogs from the 1960s, 30-year-old telephone books (stinky but still readable) and even a kitchen sink made in 1955. Seeing, and smelling, is believing.

As you tour this landfill with our intergalactic visitors, can you find things that should have been recycled? Can you suggest ways to reuse some items, for the benefit of Earthlings and intergalactic travelers alike?

THE FOUR R'S — THE WAY OF THE 2000'S

Don't leave needless garbage to confuse future garbologists. Instead:

* REDUCE: Buy what you need. Use less and choose things to last.

* REUSE: Pass on used clothes and toys. Take your own shopping bags and buy products in returnable or refillable containers.

* RECYCLE: Bottles, jars, metal cans, fine paper, newspapers, garden waste, kitchen compost and plastic containers are all recyclable.

* REFUSE: Find alternatives to toxic and corrosive cleansers. Don't buy overpackaged products.

1609
Czechoslovakia
Johann Kepler proposes that the planets revolve around the sun, not around Earth.

1610
Italy
Galileo Galilei views the night sky through a telescope and reports that Jupiter has moons and that Saturn has a ring.

1614
United States
Pocahontas (Matoaka) marries John Rolfe.

1620
United States
Settlers arrive on board the *Mayflower*.

1626
France
Dueling is declared punishable by death.

1649
England
King Charles I loses his head to the executioner.

FOOTSTEPS IN TIME

For millennia, people have used whatever is plentiful to make shoes. The first sandals were made from bark and woven grasses. In colder climates, people wrapped their feet in animal fur. Over the last two millennia, most shoes have been made of leather — the skin of the meat we eat. What will shoes be made of in the next millennium? One thing that's plentiful is garbage. Rescue some old shoes from the garbage and turn them into new slippers.

1. Cut the soles from the shoes. Then cut the soles to fit your feet. Ask an adult to help you if you are using a craft knife.

2. Glue old socks onto the soles. Where the sock meets the sole, run a line of staples for security.

3. Sew on decorations to make your personal fashion statement.

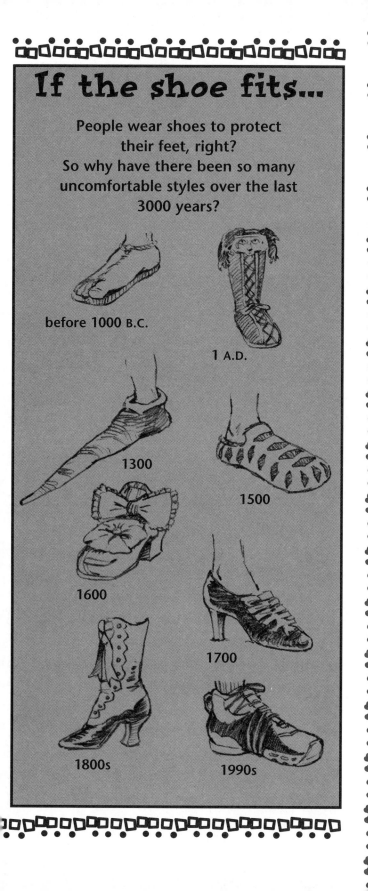

If the shoe fits...

People wear shoes to protect their feet, right?
So why have there been so many uncomfortable styles over the last 3000 years?

before 1000 B.C.

1 A.D.

1300

1500

1600

1700

1800s

1990s

1650s
Germany
Otto von Guericke's experiments with vacuums prove that animals need air to survive.

1665
England
Isaac Newton develops the theory of gravity and later says he was inspired by the fall of an apple. He also discovers that white light is made from a mixture of colors.

1670
Europe
Minute hands are added to watches.

1670
England
Aphra Benn begins her writing career. She becomes the first Englishwoman to make her living by writing.

1677
France
Ice cream becomes popular.

1680
Mauritius
The dodo bird becomes extinct.

1698
Russia
A tax is levied on men who have beards.

NEW AND IMPROVED

Heron used hidden balances, pulleys, siphons and other tricks to create his wonders.

11-year-old Bernie Yeung invented a "night writer" by taping a flashlight to a pencil. He uses it to write in his diary at night.

Teresa and Mary Thompson, aged 8 and 9, invented a solar-heated teepee called a Wigwarm.

What do the following have in common?

* a coin-operated vending machine
* a miniature steam engine
* water- and wind-powered organs
* an automatic door
* a burglar alarm

All of these items were invented as special effects to amaze people in theaters or temples. And all were invented by Heron of Alexandria, born nearly two millennia ago in Egypt. Later inventors borrowed Heron's ideas and adapted them for use in everyday life.

Today, moviemakers are developing exciting special effects such as virtual reality, digital sound and computer graphics. And again, people such as doctors, teachers, athletes and pilots are finding neat, everyday ways to use them.

Can *you* create an invention for the new millennium? Lots of kids have.

Here are some tips to get *your* inventive mind working:

* Think of something you use every day, such as a peanut butter jar, lunch box or pencil.

Katie Harding, aged 5, taped a flashlight to an umbrella, so she could sidestep puddles on dark, rainy nights.

How do you get the last of the peanut butter out of the jar? 14-year-old Jim Wollin invented a jar that opens at both ends.

* Ask yourself, does something about this object bug me? How can I make it work better? Write down all your ideas in a list — even the wacky ones.
* Are there any ideas you can borrow from existing inventions to solve your problem?
* Choose the best idea, but don't throw away the list.

You may want to go back to it later.
* Make a model and test it. Don't expect it to work perfectly the first time.
* Watch how it works or fails. How can you improve it?
* Stick at it. Consider some of the other ideas you listed. Would they help? It may take several tries to make a good invention.

1709
Italy
The piano is invented.

1714
France
The surgical syringe is invented.

1714
Germany
A mercury thermometer to measure temperature is made by Gabriel Fahrenheit. The Celsius scale is invented 28 years later by Anders Celsius.

1729
Germany
Cuckoo clocks become popular.

1736
Peru
A visiting French naturalist reports seeing "crying wood" — rubber trees oozing sap.

1749
United States
Benjamin Franklin tests a lightning rod at his home.

TIME TRAVEL

Flick open your personal telecommunicator and call for an auto taxi. In seconds, there's a beep at the loading dock of your space module. You get into the auto taxi and speak into the voice-activated navigation computer: "Take me to Katie's house." En route, mini-helicopters, butterfly spaceships and other driverless taxis whiz by at hypersonic speed. You don't have time to buckle up because you're already there.

Is that what travel will be like in the next millennium? If so, technology has a long way to go. One of the biggest problems is fuel. Fossil fuels, such as gasoline, are running out, and the alternatives of wind, sun and hydrogen are still experimental.

Fuel wasn't a big problem a millennium or two back in time. Most travel was done by sailing ships. Compasses helped sailors find their way.

The compass was invented by a Chinese inventor nearly two millennia ago. If you're thinking of taking a trip to mark the new millennium, make a Chinese compass to be sure you're headed in the right direction.

YOU WILL NEED

a small magnet

a sewing needle

a pin

a piece of thread 10 cm (4 in.) long

a pencil

a small drinking glass

1. Magnetize the needle by rubbing one end of the magnet along the needle. Stroke the magnet in the same direction 30 times. If the needle picks up a pin, it is magnetized.

2. Tie one end of the thread around the middle of the needle. Tie the other end around the middle of the pencil.

3. Place the pencil across the rim of the glass so that the needle can swing freely inside the glass. Make sure the glass is on a flat surface. The needle will point in a north-south direction.

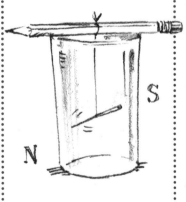

Traveler's checklist

1000 A.D.	2000 A.D.
leather sandals	cross trainers
water in a leaking skin bag	squeeze bottle filled with power juice
crust of black bread	backpack full of nutritious snacks
your own voice	portable CD player and favorite CDs
shouting from hilltops	cellular phone
caught in a thunderstorm	shelter in a fast food restaurant
dirt track	sidewalks
find the North Star	check your map
sunstroke and sunburn	baseball caps and sunscreen

1751
France
The first encyclopedia is published.

1764
Austria
Wolfgang Amadeus Mozart writes his first symphony at the age of eight.

1775
United States
The American Revolution begins with Paul Revere's ride.

1776
England and United States
The United States declares itself independent from Britain.

1779
France
Antoine Laurent Lavoisier gives the gas oxygen its name.

1792
England
Mary Wollstonecraft writes a book calling for equal education for women.

1796
England
Edward Jenner develops a successful vaccine against smallpox, a dreaded contagious disease.

PREDICT YOUR FUTURE

Imagine what you'll be like in 2050 — you will be older than your parents are now. What does your future hold?

Write down your predictions for the future and put them in an envelope marked "Do Not Open Until 2050." Store the envelope somewhere safe, perhaps in a family photo album or a box of family treasures. Then, when the year 2050 rolls around, open the envelope and see how accurate your predictions were.

* Where will I live? What will my bedroom be like?

* What will my work be?

* Will I have children? If so, what will their names be?

* Where will I go for my holidays? On Earth, on the moon?

* How will I travel?

* What will be my favorite snack food?

* What will be my favorite shows? Will there still be TV?

* What will my hobbies be?

MASH — MILLENNIUM VERSION

Want to leave your future to chance? Play this game and see what may be in store for you.

1. Draw a pentagon (a five-sided figure). Along one side of the pentagon write: Mansion, Apartment, Space Station, Hut.

2. On the other sides of the pentagon write: four possible marriage partners, four numbers, four methods of travel and four places. Now you have five categories, one along each side of the pentagon.

3. To play, choose a number between 1 and 20. Let's say you pick 15. Starting with "Mansion" as number 1, "Apartment" as number 2, and so on, count out 15 words. Cross out the fifteenth word you land on. Start with the next word and count to 15 again. Cross out the fifteenth word. Keep counting to 15 and crossing out until there is just one word left in each category.

4. Now read your fortune. "In 2050, I will live in a hut with Ivan and 11 kids and travel by pickup truck to Saturn."

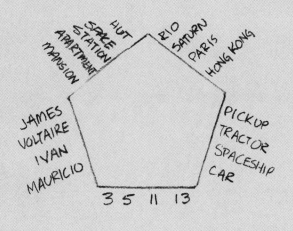

1811
England

Eleven-year-old Mary Anning discovers the first complete fossil of an ichthyosaur, an ancient creature that once lived in the sea.

1819
Switzerland

A factory produces the first chocolate bar.

1820
Antarctica

The continent of Antarctica is first sighted.

1839
Scotland

Kirkpatrick Macmillan invents the bicycle.

1842
England

Charles Darwin first explains his theory of evolution, and Richard Owen coins the word "dinosaur."

1846
United States

Baseball is first played with modern rules.

1849
United States

Blue jeans are invented.

CYBER-CELEBRATING

If you've got a computer that's hooked up to the Internet, you can celebrate the millennium in cyberspace. Explore cool websites about the millennium and send messages to the famous or the faraway.

Before you cyber-celebrate, get permission to surf the Net from the person who pays the bills. Connecting to the Internet costs money.

When you're online, keep your wits about you. Never input your full name, address or other personal information without checking with your parents first. And if you see things that make you uncomfortable, just exit.

Websites that look into past or future millennia:

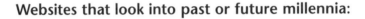

* <u>Vallon-Pont-d'Arc</u> — cave art from 17 millennia ago in France (http://www.culture.fr/culture/gvpda–en.htm)

* the <u>Seven Wonders</u> of the <u>Ancient World</u> (http://pharos.bu.edu/Egypt/Wonders/)

* the <u>Royal Ontario Museum</u> explores ancient world cultures (http://www.rom.on.ca)

* the <u>Smithsonian</u> looks backward and forward in time (http://www.si.edu)

* what's planned at <u>NASA</u>, the <u>National Aeronautics and Space Administration</u> (http://spacelink.msfc.nasa.gov/home.index.html)

* <u>Shawnee Minisink</u> — how North Americans lived 10 millennia ago (http://www.american.edu/academic.depts/cas/anthro/sms/sms.html)

Websites announcing global celebrations for the year 2000:

* <u>Sydney 2000 Olympic Games</u> in Sydney, Australia (http://www.sydney.olympic.org)

* <u>Expo 2000 Hannover</u>, the World's Fair in Hannover, Germany (http://www.expo2000.de)

E-millennium

You can send millennial e-mail messages to people you don't know — even the President of the United States (president @whitehouse.gov). Look in newspapers and magazines for e-mail addresses of sports heroes, musicians or movie and television stars. Swap addresses with friends. If you're having trouble finding e-mail addresses, try the 411 website e-mail directory (http://www.four11.com/).

Web wandering

Check out the websites on page 58. Web addresses change often, so if you can't find a site, search for the underlined key words in its name. Once at a site, try clicking on terms like "What's New," "Hot Topics" and "Fun Stuff."

1854
Russia
Florence Nightingale and her team prove the value of good nursing care in a dirty, rat-infested army hospital in the Crimea.

1866
Sweden
Alfred Nobel invents dynamite. Later, Nobel donates the money he earns from his invention to start the annual Nobel prizes.

1876
United States
Alexander Graham Bell makes the first telephone call.

1876
Belgium
French fries are eaten for the first time.

1877
United States
Thomas Edison invents the phonograph, an early kind of record player. Edison's later inventions include the lightbulb and the movie camera.

1896
Greece
The modern Olympic Games begin.

1897
France
Marie Curie studies radium and later wins a Nobel Prize for her work.

FUTURE PRESENTS

Step outside. What do you see? Buildings, trimmed lawns, cars passing? Two millennia ago, you might have stepped out into a forest of giant oaks, felt moss under your feet, and seen the flash of a fleeing deer.

Why not start a garden of plants that once grew naturally where you live. Your garden might attract small animals, birds and insects. Now there's a millennial present to the Earth!

Here's how to replant a natural garden:

1. Check the library to find out which plants grew where you live a millennium or two ago.

2. Look around your neighborhood for living examples of plants you found in your research. Collect seeds from them.

Grass and flower seeds

Let the seeds dry on the stalk, then collect them by rubbing the seed heads between your fingers. Plant in the spring or summer.

Seeds from deciduous trees and shrubs

Collect the ripe fruits but do not remove the seeds inside. Plant the whole fruits in your garden in the fall.

The fruit of the oak tree

The fruit of the maple tree

Seeds from evergreen trees

Collect unopened cones and place them on a pan in the sun. Heat will release the seeds.

Start the seeds indoors. Use a nail to poke holes in the bottom of a can. Put a few pebbles in the bottom and fill with soil. Plant one seed per can, about 1 cm (½ in.) deep and place the can on a saucer near a window (not in direct sunlight). Keep the seeds moist but not wet so seedlings will sprout. Plant your tree seedlings outside in spring.

WILDLIFE ON THE EDGE

For the thousands of species worldwide that are endangered or at risk, the new millennium could be another step toward extinction or, with help, a step in the right direction. Individuals make a difference. The lifestyle *you* choose can help preserve habitat for wildlife. Check out "The Four R's" on page 49, and see what you can do.

1903
United States
The Wright brothers make the first successful airplane flight — it lasts 12 seconds.

1912
Atlantic Ocean
The *Titanic* hits an iceberg and sinks. More than 1500 people drown.

1926
England
The first television picture shows a ventriloquist operating two dolls.

1928
United States
Walt Disney speaks (squeaks?) the part of Mickey Mouse in the first animated cartoon with sound.

1939
Europe
World War II begins.

1948
England
The first computer capable of storing a program malfunctions when a moth gets inside. Ever since, people have complained about computer "bugs."

YOUR GIFT TO THE FUTURE

A lot of good things have happened over the last two millennia. Some of the people who changed the world were famous scientists, artists, politicians, warriors, peacemakers or thinkers. But most were just ordinary folk whose combined efforts made a big difference.

Terry Fox is one example. Terry wasn't a famous person. He was an ordinary young man who had his right leg removed 15 cm (6 in.) above the knee because of bone cancer. Terry decided to run across Canada to raise money to fight cancer. He never finished his trip because his cancer reoccurred, but he raised a lot of money. And every year since his death in 1981, people have run in memory of Terry Fox and raised millions of dollars to fight cancer.

The millennium is a good time to look around for a cause YOU believe in. Here are three groups you can help by raising money. Many other organizations need money or volunteers too.

* The International Red Cross helps families after disasters such as hurricanes, floods, earthquakes, famines and wars. Contact your local Red Cross Society to find out about its disaster-relief fund or check the International website (http://www.icrc.org).

NEW MILLENNIUM EVE RESOLUTIONS

On New Year's Eve, people make resolutions to start the next year right. Since New Millennium Eve is a once-in-a-thousand-year celebration, why not make some extra-special resolutions for a better future for the world?

Think of resolutions you can make to help the environment and other people.

* Collect 2000 coins to help save wildlife.

* Tell Sis she's cool — stop using putdowns.

* Say "no" to wasteful packaging. Recycle!

* Welcome the new kid at school.

* Visit Grandpa more often.

* Help at the bake sale for flood relief.

---

* UNICEF helps make life better for children in poor countries with many projects, such as building new schools or digging wells for clean drinking water. Contact the UNICEF office in the nearest big city or visit the website (http://www.unicef.org).

* WWF, the worldwide conservation group, has a millennium campaign called The Living Planet. WWF wants to save wildlife and wild places for future people and the Earth. Contact your national WWF office to find out what you can do to help or check the international website (http://www.panda.org).

1957
Russia

The first satellite, *Sputnik-I*, is launched.

1967
South Africa

After the first human heart transplant operation, the patient lives for 18 days.

1969
Moon

NASA astronaut Neil Armstrong walks on the moon during the voyage of Apollo 11.

1989
South Africa

Helen Suzman retires from the South African parliament. For many years she was the only member of parliament to speak out against the country's racist laws.

1990
Germany

The Berlin Wall is torn down, and East and West Germany are united for the first time in 45 years.

1997
Mars

NASA's Pathfinder mission lands a robotic rover that studies the surface of the planet.

2000

World population exceeds 6 billion people.

INDEX